ONE AFTERNOON
by Yumi Heo

Orchard Books / New York

Orchard Books
95 Madison Avenue
New York, NY 10016

Manufactured in Singapore
Printed and bound by Toppan Printing Company, Inc.
Book design by Rosanne Kakos-Main

10 9 8 7 6 5 4 3 2 1

The text of this book is set in 18 point Optima.
The illustrations are oil paint, pencil, and collage reproduced in full color.

Heo, Yumi.
   One Afternoon / by Yumi Heo.
      p.   cm.
   Summary: Minho and his mother have a busy afternoon doing errands
   in the neighborhood.
      ISBN 0-531-06845-5. -- ISBN 0-531-08695-X (lib. bdg.)
      [1. Day--Fiction. 2. Neighborhood--Fiction.] I. Title.
PZ7.H41170n   1994
[E]--dc20   93-49394

For my parents

Minho liked to do errands with his mother.
One afternoon, they went to

the Laundromat to drop off their clothes

and then to the beauty salon
to get his mother's hair cut.

At the ice cream store,
Minho got a vanilla cone.

tweetle

They looked in the pet store window
at the puppies, kittens, hamsters,
and birds.

tweetle
tweetle   tweetle   tweetle

WUF

WUF

WUF

WUF

They picked up his father's shoes at the shoe repair store

WHURRA

and got food for dinner at the supermarket.

Last of all, Minho and his mother went back to the Laundromat to get the clothes they had dropped off.

Traffic was very heavy on the street

LAUNDROMAT

SHOE REPAIR

SUPERMARKET

ENTER

EXIT

STOP

vroom

honk

honk

vroom

A because of the construction.

ROAD CONSTRUCTION

Owooooooooooowo
OoOoO

A fire engine tried to get through.

vroom

honk

honk

The El train was passing by above.

Near Minho's apartment,
children were playing stickball.

Minho and his mother were very
happy to be back in their quiet home.
Minho was tired and fell asleep on
the couch. But from the bathroom…